In memory of
Alice McCrystal Duckmanton

My Hamster is a Spaceman

By Aaron Duckmanton

Illustrated by Virvalle Carvallo

My hamster is a spaceman,
it's only me that knows.
My hamster is a spaceman,
outer space is where he goes.

His spacesuit is a red one,
his rocket ship is blue.
My hamster is a spaceman,
if only people knew.

He blasts off through my rooftop,
soaring high above the trees.
My hamster is a spaceman,
take me with you please!

He's turning on the thrusters,
and breaking through the sky.
My hamster is a spaceman,
it's fun to see him fly.

He's safe inside his rocket,
flying through the milky way.
My hamster is a spaceman,
a new adventure every day.

In space there is no gravity,
he jumps and rolls around.
My hamster is a spaceman,
floating high above the ground.

He flies across the galaxy,
eats his picnic on the moon.
My hamster is a spaceman,
I hope he comes back soon.

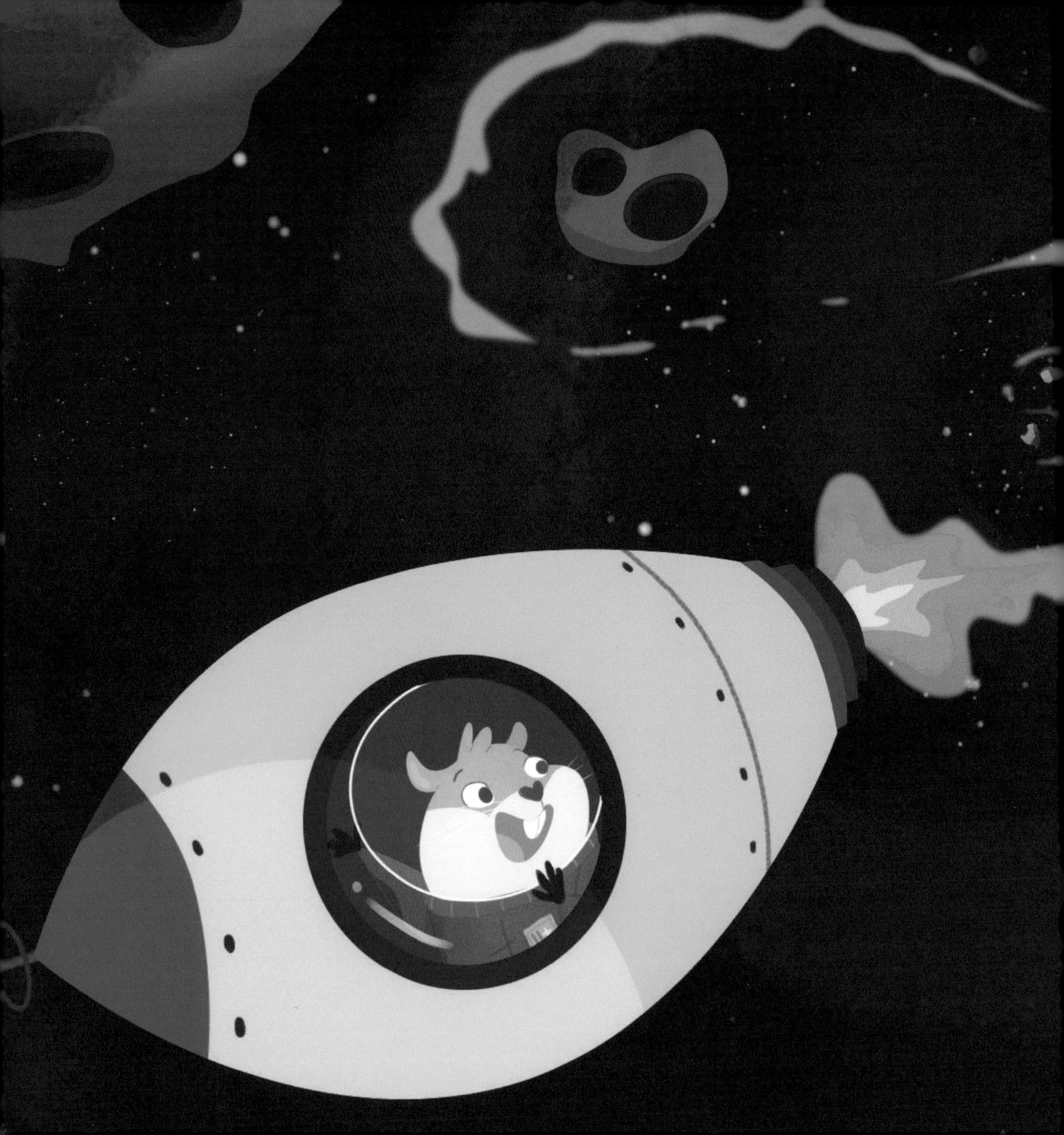

He dodges giant asteroids,
avoiding them with ease.
My hamster is a spaceman,
life in space is such a breeze.

Past Saturn and Uranus,
with all their pretty rings.
My hamster is a spaceman,
doing incredible things.

Dillon
Alfie
Ella

He's friends with all the aliens,
with skin the colour green.
My hamster is a spaceman,
oh the things he's seen!

They play hide and seek on Pluto,
and bounce around on Mars.
My hamster is a spaceman,
zooming through the stars.

They all sit down together,
as the sun begins to rise.
My hamster is a spaceman,
it's time to say goodbye.

The adventure's almost over,
he's flying on his own.
My hamster is a spaceman,
on his way back home.

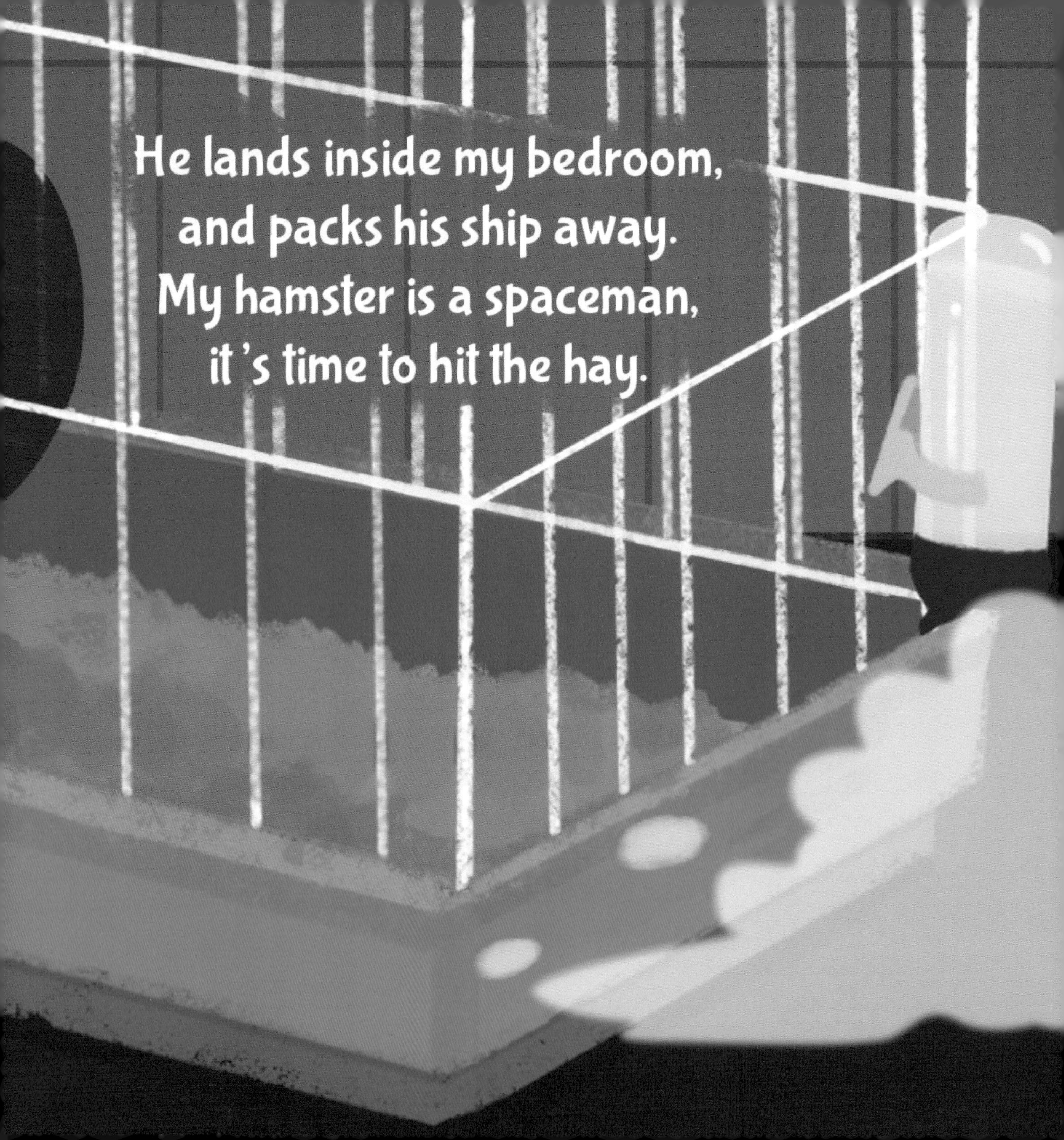

He lands inside my bedroom,
and packs his ship away.
My hamster is a spaceman,
it's time to hit the hay.

Red Planet
Planets, moon, Stars and more
The Book of
CONSTELLATIONS

I wake up and see him sleeping,
all is what it seems.
My hamster is a spaceman,
but only in my dreams...

Printed in Great Britain
by Amazon